The Amazing Adventures of Boat Girl

Written by Diane Seltzer
Illustrated by Aaron Kleger

Printed in the United States of America

ISBN-13: 978-1500550080

ISBN-10: 1500550086

To Emma and Eva, our little boat girls who were
"born & raised on the water"
- D.S.

The Amazing Adventures of Boat Girl

This book belongs to

_____

This is a story about a very brave little girl who learned to love boating.

One day the little girl's mommy and daddy told her that they had a BIG surprise...

they got a... **boat!**

Her mommy and daddy said they would go on boat rides, go swimming in the river and have all types of fun boating adventures.

The little girl was very happy and excited, but also a little scared. She had never been on a boat before and didn't know what to expect.

Maybe the boat would be rocky in the water? Or maybe she might have to swim with fish?

And then, before she went on the boat for the first time, her mommy and daddy gave her another big surprise...

....a very special life jacket for her to wear.

When she put on the life jacket she felt like she magically transformed into someone different.
She was no longer a little girl afraid to go boating.

She was... **BOAT GIRL!**

Boat Girl felt safe and secure with her "magical" jacket... and now she couldn't wait to have fun boating adventures!

She grabbed her daddy's hand as she
Jumped on board the boat and yelled...

"I am **BOAT GIRL!**"

As they cruised along the river the boat created a fountain of bubbles.

She imagined the wake was a giant lobster swimming in the water behind the boat.

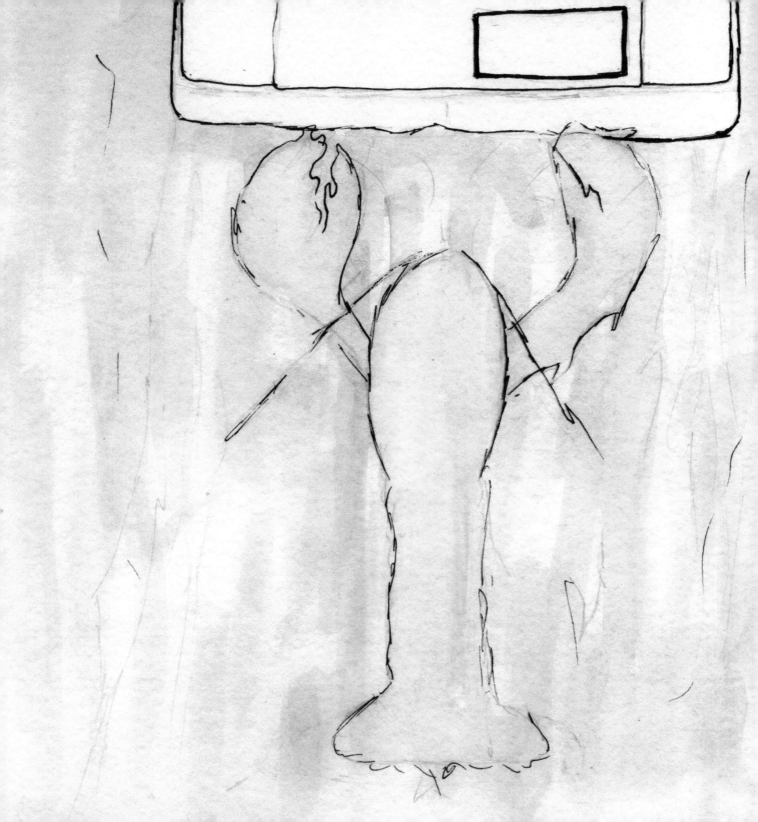

Birds soared in the sky above as if they were challenging the boat for a race.

"I am **BOAT GIRL!**" she told them.
She just knew *she* would win the race.

Other boats on the water passed by and all the passengers on board waved "Hello".

They must know that **I am Boat Girl**, she thought to herself.

When they arrived at a cove they dropped an anchor into the water to go for a swim.

The anchor sunk into the sand and held the boat in place to keep it from floating away.

Boat Girl discovered that her magical jacket helped her float in the water!

She moved her arms, kicked her feet and was swimming in the river behind the boat.

Then she heard a **SPLISH!**
Followed by a big **SPLASH!**
There were **FISH** in the water!

Boat Girl was actually swimming with the fish...
but it wasn't scary at all. It was SO much fun!

At the water's edge there was a sandy beach filled with treasures.

Boat Girl felt so lucky to be able to find all the shiniest rocks and the biggest shells.

Back on the boat it was time for lunch. Everyone was hungry from swimming... *even* the ducks!

A family of ducks swam up behind the boat and Boat Girl fed them by sprinkling crackers into the water. Boat Girl giggled as the ducks quacked and dove in the water for the crackers.

On the cruise back to the marina Boat Girl watched the late afternoon sun sparkle on the water.

The sun was starting to set and the sky was turning beautiful pink and orange colors.

It was the perfect way to end such a perfect day.

What an amazing day on the water!

Boat Girl couldn't wait to discover what **amazing** boating adventures she would have next!

Boat Girl's Safety Rules

Boat Girl learned that being **safe** was the best way to have fun on the water.

Here are some of her boating rules that you should follow too!

1. Always wear your life jacket when walking on the dock.
2. Always wear your life jacket and hold onto an adult's hand when boarding a boat.
3. Always wear your life jacket when going on a boat ride.
4. Always stay seated when docking or cruising.
5. Always wear your life jacket swimming in the river, lake or bay.
6. Always swim with an adult.
7. Always wear sunscreen and drink lots of water when spending the day in the sun.

Fun Boat Terms

Want to learn the ropes? Here are some boating terms
that every little skipper should know!

Outside the Boat

Bow or forward – front of the boat
Aft or stern – back of the boat
Port – left side of the boat
Starboard – right side of the boat
Hull – body of a boat
Beam – width of the boat
Cockpit – back deck of the boat
Cleat – metal hook on boat to tie rope to
Helm – where captain "drives" the boat

Inside the Boat

Cabin – inside part of the boat
Salon – a boat's "living room"
Stateroom – a boat's "bedroom"
Head – a boat's "bathroom"
Galley – a boat's "kitchen"

Using the Boat

Lines – ropes to tie up a boat
Underway – a moving boat
Navigation – how to safely "drive" the boat
Buoy – road signs on water
Wake – waves made by boat in water
Channel – deep waterway for boats
Raft-up – tying boats together on the water

My Boating Adventures

My Name: _____

My first boat trip was with:

_____

I was _____ years old. It was a ☐ powerboat ☐ sailboat.

Where I went boating:

_____

Things I love most about boating:

_____

_____

_____

About the Author

Diane Seltzer is the editor/founder of several boating lifestyle websites – BoaterLifeOnline.com and BoaterKids.com – where she often writes about her kids and their love of boating. A boater for over 15 years, she spends weekends on the Chesapeake Bay in Maryland with her husband and two daughters (the inspirations for this book).

Diane is also active in the boating industry as the marketing director for SureShade, makers of retractable sunshade systems for boats, and editor/founder of a collaborative marine marketing website called MarineMarketingTools.com.

About the Illustrator

Aaron Kleger is a multi-talented young man who created all of the water color drawings for this book. Specializing in pastels, watercolor and oil painting, his artwork has been honored with several awards in his school.

In addition to his artwork, he enjoys playing the guitar & clarinet, cooking, gardening and is an active boy scout.

Aaron hopes to one day become an aerospace engineer.

Made in the USA
Lexington, KY
07 December 2016

They took the boat for a cruise and Boat Girl watched in amazement as the water splashed up against the side of the boat.